THREADS

ReadZone Books Limited
www.ReadZoneBooks.com

© in this edition 2016 ReadZone Books Limited

This print edition published in cooperation with Fiction Express, who first published this title in weekly instalments as an interactive e-book.

FICTION EXPRESS

Fiction Express
First Floor Office, 2 College Street,
Ludlow, Shropshire SY8 1AN
www.fictionexpress.co.uk

Find out more about Fiction Express on pages 81–82.

Design: Laura Durman & Keith Williams
Cover Images: Shutterstock

© in the text 2014 Sharon Gosling
The moral right of the author has been asserted.

ISBN 978-1-78322-557-6

Printed in Malta by Melita Press.

THREADS

BY SHARON GOSLING

What do other readers think?

Here are some comments left on the Fiction Express blog about this book:

"I love Threads *it is epic."*
Jose, Shrewsbury

"I have really enjoyed Threads*, so thank you."*
Jack, Coventry

*"*Threads *is an amazing book and I would love to read more. It is constantly gripping you in and taking you back in time!"*
Zoe, Leicestershire

"I read Threads*. I think it is a superb book and I want to know what is going to happen in the next chapter."*
Alfie, Shrewsbury

"We have just finished reading Threads *and we really enjoyed the fantastic story!"*
Miss Yorke's Y3 & 4 Class, Allesley Primary School, Coventry.

"Oh I just read the last chapter of Threads*. It is ace. Well done Sharon you are my favourite author!!"*
Anya, Shrewsbury

Contents

For Oli and Sam

Chapter 1

Another Long Day

"Oi!" yelled a voice behind Charlie. "Stop dawdling and get on with it or I'll dock your pay, you little wretch!"

"Sorry sir!" Charlie shouted, as he hurried across the mill floor. He didn't bother to look up – he knew it was William, the owner's eldest son. It wasn't William's job to watch the workers, but he liked to do it anyway.

Charlie headed for the furthest mule, the spinning machine that had almost filled the bobbins he put on an hour ago.

He had one of the big empty reels under each arm and another wedged under his chin. He could feel a bead of sweat on his forehead. It began to trickle down his face, but he didn't have a hand free to wipe it away. Around him, scraps of white cotton floated through the hot air like soft snow, getting up his nose, sticking to his skin and tickling his ears.

Charlie glanced at the windows high above him. They were always closed, however hot it got. One gust of wind from outside would have sent thousands more cotton scraps into the air and they'd clog the machines. But how he wished for just one, small breeze! Charlie felt another dribble of sweat working its way down his neck, and sighed as he scurried on.

"You're cutting it fine," Mary yelled, over the loud, never ending clatter-clitter-clatter-rattle-thunk of the machines. "Another two minutes and we'd be done for!"

Mary looked after spinning mules one, two and three. Two years older than Charlie, she enjoyed bossing him about (as if he wasn't pushed around by everyone else enough already), but Charlie still liked her. Mary only had nine-and-a-half fingers. She'd lost part of the little finger on her left hand when it had got stuck trying to fix one of the machines.

Number one mule rattled on as Charlie lined up his empty bobbins in front of the ones that were very nearly full. He and Mary watched, waiting until the last piece of neatly spun yarn had passed over the mule and on to the bobbin. Then Mary quickly hauled up the lever, and the machine rattled to a stop. Fast as they could, the two of them pulled off the full bobbins and pushed on the empty ones. In less than thirty seconds, Mary had thrown the lever back and the mule was running again. Charlie breathed out in relief. At least William wouldn't have an excuse to cut his pay this time.

Charlie heard Mary coughing hard as he hauled up the three full bobbins. He watched as she put a hand on her chest, her hot face turning even redder. It was the bits of cotton in the air – they clogged you up until there was no room left for breath. She waved him away as he watched her, worried.

"Get on with it – number two'll need doffing right soon," she managed to rasp.

Charlie struggled with the heavy bobbins, his back aching as it always did by the end of the day. It was 6 o'clock, so there were two more hours until the shift finished. He added the full bobbins to the pile and then picked up two more empties, ready to doff the next mule. As he lifted the third, he took a deep breath. A scrap of cotton got sucked into his throat and he, too, started to cough, almost dropping the lot.

* * *

The mill shut down at 8 pm and everyone filed out, exhausted, into the January chill. Away from the spinning sheds, real snow lay thick on the ground and the air was freezing. Charlie didn't have a coat. As an extra layer his mum had given him one of his dad's old shirts to wear. Though threadbare, it was better than nothing.

Charlie found his old wooden clogs in the pile that the spinning shed workers had left outside when they arrived. They were very old and scuffed, but without them Charlie would have been walking home barefoot. The stiff, wet wood hurt his aching toes as he pushed them on, but he was used to it. He headed for the mill gates, his clogs crunching over the new snow, pushing it up to bite coldly at his bare ankles.

"Psst!"

The sound came from the shadows outside one of the coal sheds that fed the mill's great steam engine.

"Charlie! Over here!"

Charlie knew at once who it was – Clara, the mill owner's daughter. He glanced around to make sure no one was watching, and then went to say hello. Clara grinned at him from inside her thick black wool coat, and held out a twist of paper.

"What is it?" Charlie asked.

"Cook made cinder toffee," Clara said. "I saved you some."

Charlie's stomach rumbled at the mention of food. He unwrapped the paper and stuffed a piece into his mouth. "Thanks," he murmured, his mouth full.

Clara shrugged. She was always bringing him things to eat, even though it would get them both into trouble if anyone found out. They weren't supposed to be friends, as he was just one of her father's workers. When she was grown up, she'd be married off to someone rich and spend her days ordering servants about and planning parties. Charlie would most likely be working in the mill for the rest of his short life.

They had met when Clara's mother had been taken ill. Charlie's mum was paid to care for Clara and her baby brother, Edwin.

Charlie had liked Clara straight away – she was funny… and she loved climbing trees. They had stayed friends even after Charlie had started work in the mill. But they had to keep their friendship a secret. Clara's parents, Ernest and Mrs Stanton, had made it clear that they didn't think Charlie was suitable company.

"Won't they be looking for you?" Charlie asked, mumbling between chews of his toffee.

Clara shrugged. "They think I'm playing in my bedroom, but I managed to creep out through the kitchen. Father's not here anyway – he went to Manchester to see about the new equipment. They're bringing it in tonight."

"Look Clara, I'm sorry, but I've got to go," Charlie mumbled, shivering slightly in the cold night air. "Mum'll be wondering where I am and my brother will eat my tea given half a chance! Thanks for the toffee though."

Clara scowled at him. "I never see you any more, Charlie. It's so boring without you. All they let me do is sew and play the piano. I need an adventure!"

Charlie sighed, too tired to argue. "Look, maybe we can meet up on Sunday?"

"Great," said Clara, beaming. "I'll see you here at 11 o'clock."

Charlie slipped out of the coal shed and trudged home.

Chapter 2

Bad, Bad News

Charlie lived with his mum and dad, his older brother Jim, and his little sister, Liza. The family had two rooms on the lower floor of a tiny house in the town that surrounded the mill. The children slept in one room, and the other small room was both the living area and kitchen. Late at night, once the children had gone to bed, Charlie's mum and dad would pull out the old mattress that was rolled up in the corner, and sleep in front of the stove.

"Where've you been?" His mum asked, as he came in. Her face was red raw and she looked tired. "I managed to get some bacon today, and I was about to give yours to Jim."

"Sorry," Charlie muttered, taking a seat at the table and starting to eat.

Mum turned to Charlie's dad, who was still finishing his stew. "And he's really bringing one of them here?" she asked. "Stanton's not content with paying us next to nothing already – he's going to put us out of work completely."

"What's going on?" Charlie whispered to Jim, who was sitting next to him, a glum look on his face.

"Old Stanton's getting in a new type of spinning machine," his brother whispered back. "It's supposed to do the work of ten men, so they say."

"It'll be the end of us," worried Charlie's mum. "We'll all starve."

"Don't fret, Flora, love," said Charlie's dad, reaching out to put his hand over hers. "Old Stanton's not so bad, you know that. Let's just wait and see what happens, shall we?"

Charlie's mum pulled her hand away. "It's no good, Arthur," she said. "This new machine will be bad news, I'm sure of it. Bad, bad news."

Charlie went to bed worrying about the new machine and what it would mean for the mill. If it could do the work of ten people, that meant nine people who had once had jobs wouldn't be needed any more. What if he was one of them? They only had enough money coming in to have meat once a week, and that was with all of them working at the mill. Even little Liza had a job cleaning the machines.

***

Charlie woke with a start to a loud banging on the door. He peered out of the grimy window, but all he could see was pitch darkness – it must still be the middle of the night!

"What is it?" Charlie asked, as Liza, scared, began to cry. "What's happening?"

"I don't know," Jim replied grimly, as he scrambled out of bed.

The banging went on as Charlie got up. He heard his dad calling out, telling whoever it was to hold on a minute, he was just coming…. Then there was a splintering sound as the front door was kicked open and their mum screamed in fright. Jim and Charlie peered out of their bedroom in time to see several town constables barging into the cramped kitchen.

"Arthur Thwaite?" Barked one, grabbing Charlie's dad by the arm.

"Yes – what's this about?" he asked. "I don't–"

"We are arresting you for the wilful destruction of property belonging to Stanton's Cotton Mill," boomed the policeman. "You'll be coming with us now."

Charlie's mum screamed again.

Chapter 3

The Witness

Charlie and Jim ran into the room to find his dad being held by two big policemen. His mum was crouching in the corner, looking horrified.

"Let him go," Jim shouted.

"Stay back," warned one of the constables, as they began to drag Arthur Thwaite away. "We don't want any more trouble here."

"Wait!" Charlie said, "Wait – father!"

"It's all right, son," said Arthur, twisting to look back over his shoulder. "Just a misunderstanding. I'll be back in no time."

The policemen pulled Arthur from the house. Outside, the commotion had woken most of the street. Small, grimy windows framed worried faces, and a handful of neighbours and friends came out into the early morning darkness.

"That's Arthur Thwaite!" shouted one. "He's done nowt wrong all his livelong day!"

"What's happening?" demanded another, "Where are you taking him?"

The hubbub grew as the police struggled to make their way through the growing throng. "Stand back!" One of them shouted. "Or you'll all be under arrest."

An angry murmur rippled through the air, but the crowd parted enough to let the policemen and their prisoner through. Charlie darted after them. His mum called out to him, but he didn't listen. He had to find out what was going on.

The police station was right in the middle of Hewton. Charlie hurried through the narrow, dingy streets, wrapping his arms around himself against the cold, and trying to keep quiet in his wooden clogs.

When he got to the police station, a small crowd had gathered outside. Charlie recognized some of the men and women that he worked with, but others were unfamiliar. He assumed they were workers from Mercer's – the other mill on the outskirts of town.

"Charlie!" exclaimed a man called Ned. "What are you doing here?"

"I had to find out what was happening to father," Charlie said. "They just dragged him away for no reason. Do you know what's going on?"

Ned scowled. "Well, you might have heard that Stanton was bringing in a new machine tonight. The coward wouldn't do it by daylight," he spat. "He was too worried we'd down tools when we saw it. Now, rumour has it the cart carrying this machine was stopped on the road. Overturned and burned, so the story goes."

"What – and the police think that my dad did it?"

"I'm afraid so," said Ned, patting him on the shoulder.

"He'd never do anything like that!" Charlie cried. "Anyway – he was at home last night… with us!"

"Trouble is, they say they've got a witness," explained Ned.

"Then they're lying!" Charlie said, fiercely.

"We know, Charlie – that's why we're all here," Ned explained.

"Something's not right here and we're not going to stand for it. Not any more," shouted Henry, another mill worker. "Are we lads… lasses?"

An angry cheer rose up from the mob. A moment later, the doors of the police station flew open to reveal a large, red-faced sergeant.

"Right, you lot," he barked. "That's enough."

Two constables rushed out behind him and grabbed hold of Henry. "You're under arrest," one of them said.

"Wh– what for?" Henry blustered as they manhandled him towards the door.

"Starting a riot," Charlie heard one of the policemen reply as they dragged Henry inside the building.

"Anyone else?" the sergeant bellowed. "We've got cells enough to hold you all. D'you all want to lose your jobs?"

That was the final blow. There were a few angry shouts, but one by one the men and women shuffled away. All of them had families to feed, and none of them could afford to be out of work.

Ned tapped Charlie on the shoulder. "Come on, lad," he said.

"Wait," Charlie said, shaking him off and running to the steps where the policeman stood. "Who says it's my father who did this?" He asked. "Who?"

The policeman looked down at him and sniffed. "Go on – hop off home. Your poor mam doesn't need any more trouble, does she?"

"Can we see him?" Charlie asked. "If we come tomorrow, can we see my dad?"

"What, on a Sunday? You must be joking," the policeman snorted as he turned away.

Disappointed, Charlie began the long walk home, blending quietly into the cold shadows.

Chapter 4

A Suspect

Because the next day was Sunday, the mills were closed and the whole town had the day off to go to church. Charlie's mum and Liza had cried all night and neither Jim nor Charlie had slept much, but still they went along.

Once the mill workers were all seated at the back of the church, the rich families of the town walked down to their seats at the front. The Stantons sat on one side and the Mercers on the other. They weren't friends – after all, when Frederick Mercer had built his new mill, he had taken work – and workers – from Ernest Stanton.

Charlie watched through blurred eyes as they all walked past in their finery. The men were in suits of grey or black, and carried fine top hats. The ladies were in full gowns, wrapped in wool and fur to keep out the morning cold.

Charlie noticed that Clara had another new coat – blue wool, this time, with a white fur trim. She looked around for him as she always did, grinning when she spotted him in his pew. Today, he couldn't manage to smile back.

The sermon was about the perils of drink and the need for humility in all things. Charlie wasn't really listening. He was thinking up a plan to help his dad. What he needed to do was to find out who really had destroyed the machine. But first, he had to discover who this supposed witness was. Charlie knew just the person to help him, too. She was sitting at the front of the church, in a nice new blue wool coat.

After church, Charlie headed to the coal sheds to wait for Clara. At first he thought she wasn't coming. Perhaps she'd forgotten their arrangement? Then finally she appeared and they headed to their 'secret place' – an oak tree that grew in one of the fields behind Stanton's mill. It was so old that at some point a lightning strike had cleaved it in two. The tree had carried on growing around the split to create a woody cavern that could only be seen if you were right up close to it.

Charlie hoisted himself inside and Clara clambered after him. She was still wearing her new coat, but didn't seem at all bothered about getting it dirty.

"What's going on?" she asked. "You didn't even smile at me in church. Why are you so grumpy?"

"Haven't you heard?" Charlie asked. "Dad's been arrested for destroying your father's stupid new machine."

"No!" Clara gasped. "So it was your father! Papa's so angry about that. It cost so much money and it will take *months* to get a new one! Why would he do such a thing?" she asked, her eyes wide.

"He didn't do it, Clara," Charlie snapped. "But to prove that, I've got to find out who did. They say they've got a witness. But whoever it is must be lying, because father was at home all night. Will you help me?"

Clara nodded thoughtfully. "Of course I will. We must be able to work it out. Has your dad got any enemies?"

Charlie frowned. "No, everyone loves him!"

Clara shrugged. "There must be someone he's argued with? Someone he got into trouble?"

Charlie racked his brains but shook his head. "My dad doesn't argue with anyone, and he wouldn't get anyone in trouble. He's always trying to help people, and–" he stopped.

Clara raised her eyebrows at him. "And?"

"No – he wouldn't!"

"Who wouldn't what? Come on, Charlie, talk sense."

Charlie shook his head. "About a year ago, father stopped this man called Jack Hoggett from stealing firewood from the mill. He didn't report him, but your brother William found out and Hoggett was fired anyway. He came to our house, shouting that my dad had ratted on him."

"There you go, then," Clara said, taking two apples from her pocket and passing one to Charlie. "Sounds like a suspect to me."

"But that was ages ago! And it wasn't father's fault! He went round to Hoggett's house to explain and make amends."

"Well it's a place to start, isn't it?" Clara said, standing up and scrambling out of the tree. "Come on."

"Where are we going?" Charlie sputtered around a mouthful of fruit.

"To Jack Hoggett's house! We're going to need some proof, so let's go and find some!"

* * *

Jack Hoggett and his wife Nettie lived in a small house on the other side of town. They shared with three other families, and had one upstairs room of the two-storey dwelling.

"How is this going to help us?" Charlie asked, looking up at it from where they were crouched in an alley. "We're not going to be able to get inside, are we?"

Clara looked around, and then pointed to a wall that ran right beside the house on the left. "If we climb on to that, we'll be able to listen at the window."

Charlie frowned. "I don't know if that's a good idea. What if–"

Clara interrupted. "We haven't got time to argue," she said, briskly. "Do you want to help your dad, or not?"

Charlie bit his lip and nodded. Together they crossed the street and began climbing the wall, using the uneven bricks as handholds. It was higher than Charlie had realized, but Clara didn't seem bothered. When they reached the top, he tried not to look down as they edged along to the house and crouched by the Hoggetts' tiny window.

"What have you done?" Came a woman's worried voice, from inside the room. "Oh, Jack! You could swing for this!"

"It won't be me that's hanging, Nettie," said Jack Hoggett, "And neither will Arthur Thwaite. They'll transport him is all."

"But his family – his children!"

"Thwaite didn't think of *my* family, *my* children when he GOT me fired, did he now?"

"But Jack–"

There was a sudden scraping sound, followed by the clomp of boots on wood. Charlie realized that someone was moving to the window. If they looked out, the two of them would be discovered. Charlie grabbed Clara's arm.

"Clara, we've got to go," he said.

"No, wait," she hissed. "He hasn't said for sure it was him yet! We've got to stay!"

"But if they see us–"

Charlie didn't manage to finish his sentence, because then something terrible happened.

Chapter 5

Caught!

"You!"

Charlie felt someone grasp his leg and yelled in surprise as he almost overbalanced and fell from the wall. He grabbed hold of Clara to try and stop himself and looked down to see her older brother standing right below them. William looked very angry.

"Get down here, you," he growled, as Charlie continued to struggle.

"William!" Clara squeaked, trying to keep her voice down so that the Hoggetts wouldn't hear. "What are you doing here?"

"Let me go!" Charlie hissed, trying to shake William off, but it was no good. Clara's brother pulled him until he slid off the wall and dropped to the ground. Clara followed, getting even more dirt all over her new coat as she scrabbled down.

"William!" Clara said, again, as her brother grabbed Charlie by the shoulders. "Leave him alone!"

"What on earth do you think you are doing with… with *him*?" William demanded. "Running away, climbing walls in your Sunday best? Mother and father have got the whole household out looking for you! Did *he* make you do this?"

As he said the word 'he', William shook Charlie so hard that his teeth clattered together. Clara darted forwards, pushing her brother away.

"Charlie didn't do anything! If you *must* know, we're… we're investigating a crime," said Clara, angry too.

"Crime?" William sneered. "What crime?"

Clara stood beside Charlie, crossing her arms and lifting her chin defiantly. "We're finding out who really destroyed papa's machine."

"We know who did it," William hissed, pointing at Charlie. "It was *his* father."

"No, it wasn't," said Charlie, hotly. "And we're going to prove it by finding the real criminal."

"Our first suspect is Jack Hoggett," explained Clara.

"What's Hoggett got to do with it?" William spat. "He doesn't even work for us any more."

"We know that!" Clara said, stamping her foot impatiently.

"Well, why should he care about our new machine then?" said William, just as impatiently. "He's at Mercer's now. He's nothing to do with us at all."

Clara and Charlie looked at each other. Jack Hoggett worked for Frederick Mercer? They hadn't known that!

Before either of them could say anything else, William grabbed Charlie by the arm again. "Hey!" Charlie protested. "What are you doing? I haven't done anything wrong, let me go!"

"I don't know what you're up to, boy," snarled William, "but I *do* know my father will want to hear how you persuaded his favourite daughter to run around with you like a ragamuffin. So I think it'd be best if you came back to the house with me. Then you can explain yourself, can't you?"

Chapter 6

The Big House

Clara's house was a large, square brick building right in the centre of Stanton's mill complex. It had three storeys and a steep set of steps leading up to big, black double doors at the front. Charlie had never walked up the steps to the main entrance before. When he'd come with his mother as a little boy, they'd always used the kitchen entrance around the back – just like all the other servants. He hesitated at the bottom, looking up at the imposing black doors. He suddenly felt very nervous.

"Get a move on," William said, yanking his arm. Clara scowled at her brother, but didn't say anything.

Inside, the floor was made of oak boards that had been polished until they shone. There was a wide, sweeping staircase that led from the main hall up to the second floor. As they entered, a smartly-dressed butler appeared.

"Ahh, Minton," said William, in his most grandiose tone. "Get my father, would you?"

Mr Stanton appeared a few minutes later. A tall gentleman with grey hair and a thin face, he looked relieved when he saw his daughter.

"Where have you been?" he asked Clara, when she ran over to him. "Your mother has been so worried!" He peered over her head and frowned as he saw Charlie. "And who's this?"

William spoke before Clara had a chance to. "This is Charlie Thwaite – the son of the man who wrecked your new spinner, father."

"He didn't!" Charlie and Clara shouted at the same time.

"Papa, we've been trying to prove that Charlie's father isn't the one who broke your machine," Clara explained. "You see, there's a man called Jack Hoggett, and–" She began to tell him how Hoggett had argued with Charlie's dad, and that they had decided to go to Hoggett's house to investigate. At first, Charlie thought it was going well, but when Clara described the eavesdropping, her father frowned and began to shake his head. Charlie's heart sank.

When Clara had finished her tale, Mr Stanton turned to Charlie. "And I suppose this was all *your* idea, boy?

Encouraging my daughter to climb walls and listen at windows?"

"No, that was my suggestion, father!" Clara insisted, tugging desperately on his arm, "Please listen to me – Jack Hoggett works at Mercer's mill, and–"

"That's enough," said Ernest Stanton firmly. "You will stop all this nonsense right away. Do you really believe that you know better than the police?"

"No, father… well, it's just…" Clara spluttered.

"Hoggett has identified Arthur Thwaite as the criminal," Mr Stanton thundered. "Now this cunning young wretch is trying to turn your head. It's simply a matter of revenge."

"No, that's not so!" Clara shouted. "Charlie's not cunning at all! He's… he's my friend."

"Well, not any more," said Stanton. "Clara, as my daughter, you have standards to uphold. You will not see this boy again." As Clara opened her mouth to beg, Stanton held up his hand. "It won't do, my girl. Do you understand?"

"Yes, father," said Clara, bowing her head.

The mill owner turned to look at Charlie so gravely that his heart began to thump and a horrible, uneven sick feeling bubbled in his stomach. "As for you, Thwaite, I must say I'm disappointed. Your father has worked for me for many years, and I always thought he was a good man. It seems I was mistaken. And now *you* are brought before me, leading my daughter astray and causing me more trouble."

Charlie suddenly realized what was about to happen. "Please sir," he said, "I'm sorry, I–"

"With that in mind, I can no longer employ you at Stanton's mill. Collect your final pay tomorrow."

"No!" Charlie cried. "Please, Mr Stanton! You can't sack me – with father in jail, that means two of us out of work! We'll starve – we won't be able to pay the rent!"

William smirked. "You should have thought about that before you got my sister involved in your little scheme," he sneered.

"William! Be quiet!" Clara shouted. "Father, please don't dismiss Charlie! Please!"

"My decision is made, Clara," said her dad. "It's for the best."

"Wait," Charlie begged, "Mr Stanton–"

The mill owner held up his hand. "There will be no more discussion, boy. Your family's financial worries are nothing to do with me. For now, I'll allow your mother and siblings to continue at the mill… but if there's any more trouble, they'll be given their marching orders. Do you understand?"

"Yes… sir," Charlie mumbled.

With that, Mr Stanton turned on his heel and led Clara away. She looked over her shoulder as she went. "I'm sorry, Charlie!" she said, sounding tearful. "I'm so sorry!"

"Go on," said William, pushing him towards the door. "If you're not off the property in five minutes, I'll call the constable. Then you can join your *dear* father in jail, how would you like that?"

Charlie felt like crying himself. He walked through the doors and down the steps, crossing the mill courtyard for the last time. When he got to the gate he turned and looked back at Clara's window. He could see her standing there, waving at him, but he didn't wave back.

* * *

Charlie couldn't bear to tell his ma and Jim and Liza what had happened. Instead, after a fitful night, he got up as usual the next morning, and went to Stanton's mill to collect the final wages he'd been promised. It was cold, and he shivered as he walked, wondering miserably what on earth he was going to do next. He had to find a job, somehow – anything would do.

As he reached the mill gates, he heard the sound of loud voices. A group of angry men had gathered outside the spinning sheds, talking and shouting among themselves. Charlie saw Ned at the edge of the crowd.

"What's happening?" he asked.

"Stanton's got another machine coming in," Ned grumbled. "We won't stand for it, lad – we won't! We're going to form a union. These men here – we're the best workers he's got. We're walking out, right now. Let's see how long he can last without us. He'll be begging us to come back and forgetting about these blasted machines in no time! We'll show them, Charlie – they need us! Come on!"

"I can't!" Charlie said. "Stanton dismissed me yesterday, but... but maybe he'll ask me back if you're all out on strike. I need the work, Ned!"

Ned shook his head. "You'll get no sympathy from this lot if you work for Stanton today," he warned. Then, seeing Charlie's look of dismay, he dropped his voice to a whisper. "I've heard they need doffers, up at Mercer's. Why don't you go up there and ask for work? Better than working here. Or just come to the meeting with me now – maybe we can work something out."

The angry group began to move away, heading for the gates. Ned went with them, leaving Charlie wondering what to do next. If he went through those gates to work, he'd be branded a strike-breaker forever, but it would prove his loyalty to Mr Stanton. If he went to Mercer's, he'd be working for the 'enemy'. What would Clara think? What would his own family think? But, if he joined the strike, he might not get a job anywhere, ever again. On the other hand, he might be able to find out some useful information about the night the machine was damaged. What was he to do?

Chapter 7

An Unexpected Discovery

The men's angry voices faded away as they disappeared around the corner. Still Charlie hesitated, looking back towards the big house. He could see Mr Stanton watching from one of the big upstairs windows, his hands clasped behind his back. The memory of Clara clinging to her father's arm, begging him not to dismiss her friend, swam before Charlie's eyes.

Charlie's mind was made up. He turned and headed for the mill gates, hurrying through the town after the men. As they walked, Charlie tried to work out where the meeting was being held, and then realized that they were making for the small hall under the clock-tower. It was run by the local vicar, but when they got there, the little man looked worried and wouldn't let them in.

"I don't want any trouble," Charlie could hear him saying. "You know Mr Stanton pays for this place! You'll have to stay out here for your meeting."

An angry grumble ran through the throng of people, which had doubled in size since they had left Stanton's mill. Most of them were men, but there were some women and children, too – all as shabbily dressed as Charlie. He looked around the crowd, remembering how grand Mr Stanton's house had been. He knew that most of the people here would never even get to touch anything as expensive as the mill owner's *boots*. The thought made him angry and sad at the same time.

"Friends," boomed a voice rising over the hubbub. A big, burly man stood on the steps of the hall, in front of its closed door. Charlie recognized him as Jonas Tripp, the man who ran Stanton's steam engine. The crowd hushed, listening to what he had to say. "We're all here for the same reasons. Because we've had enough of how men who think they are our betters treat us all the days of our lives."

A murmur of agreement rippled through the waiting crowd.

"I say, enough is enough," Tripp continued. "We make these men money. We make them what they are. It's time they repaid us."

The mutterings became shouts of agreement. And then someone yelled, "How, Jonas? How do we do make them pay?"

"By hitting them where it really hurts!" Tripp shouted back. "By downing tools and refusing to work until they pay us what we're worth! Until they pay us enough to feed our families properly! Until they pay us enough to get as fat as they are! Until they realize they can't replace *us* with machines. Until they respect us the way we should be respected!"

The crowd was cheering and clapping now, yells of assent filling the small square. Charlie looked around at the red, tired faces, but didn't feel like cheering himself. He couldn't see how refusing to work was going to help any of them. Usually, when someone couldn't work – because they were sick, perhaps, or had been injured –

then the others would chip in and give them a few pennies, or something to eat, just to tide them over until they could go back to work. Otherwise their families would starve. But what would happen if no one was getting paid? Who would help them then?

"And don't worry about your loss of pay," boomed Tripp, as if he'd read Charlie's thoughts. "Those of you who are already registered members will receive strike pay, paid by the union. Those of you who aren't members – you just need to join up."

"Strike pay t'aint much!" yelled back one voice.

"It's better than nowt," countered Tripp. "This won't be easy, for sure, but it's for the best. We have to think about our future! It's time to make a stand."

There was another round of cheering, although it was more subdued now. Then Charlie saw another movement at the front of the crowd. Another man had got up beside Tripp. It was Jack Hoggett! Charlie clenched his hands in anger. Hoggett had a quick word with Tripp, who nodded and then let him take his place.

"I've got another suggestion," he said, once the crowd had settled enough to hear him. "You don't have to rely on the union. They ain't the answer. They'll take your money and sure, you'll get strike pay – but that's hardly enough for a loaf of bread a day, is it? And how long will it last, eh?"

The crowd worried aloud, muttering to each other, nodding and shaking their heads.

"But if you go to Mercer's," Hoggett continued, "they're willing to take on any who'll turn up. Mr Mercer's not a hard task-master like Stanton."

"Oh yeah?" shouted a voice. "How much does he pay?"

"Not as much as you'd have got at Stanton's, but more than you'll get with strike pay," Hoggett shouted back. "And it won't run out, neither. Mr Mercer's expanding his business. Once he's got more workers, he can take more orders, see? Then he can put up wages. But he *don't* like unions. So my advice is to forget this strike and find employment elsewhere – that's even more of a blow for Stanton!"

Hoggett left the stage, nodding at Tripp as he went. The crowd descended into a rabble of noise again, as Tripp tried to speak, but Charlie wasn't listening anyway. He was more interested in Jack Hoggett. He followed the man as he slipped quietly out of the square and made his way through a series of quiet streets to the edge of town. There he met with another man who was well-dressed and portly.

Charlie's jaw dropped.

Chapter 8

The Plot

There, just a few yards from Charlie, stood Frederick Mercer himself! The mill owner was leaning on a polished black cane beside a gate that led up into the town park. Hoggett began to speak to him as Charlie hid behind the wide trunk of an oak tree to listen.

"Well?" Mercer asked.

"It's done. It might take a few days, but once they all run out of money, they'll come running to you. The strike pay they're offering isn't enough to feed a cat."

The mill owner smiled, his teeth showing through his fat jowls. "Good. Let's see how long Stanton can last without any workers. I know for a fact he's got three orders that need filling by next month. Once he misses those, his name will be mud throughout the industry. It won't be long until he closes."

"And once he does?" Hoggett asked. "What about the workers' wages? Will you put them up, like you said?"

Mercer looked him up and down. "What do you care? You're being paid enough, aren't you?"

Hoggett hesitated, and then shrugged. "Sorry sir, t'aint my business," he muttered. Then he added, more loudly, "My contact tells me Stanton's got another machine coming in tonight. That might keep him going a while longer – even if he has to run it himself."

A black look crossed Mercer's face. "Do you know the route they're taking?"

"It's coming in over the marshes at Markwell Cross and down through Mowton, so I heard."

"Burn it. And this time, make sure the blame falls on that union fellow – what's his name, Tripp? We don't need troublemakers like him in this town."

"Yes, sir," replied Hoggett.

"And meet them at the Cross this time," Mercer went on. "That way it'll be a nasty surprise."

Hoggett nodded and left. Charlie had to crouch down quickly to avoid being seen. His heart was racing. He had to do something! If he could have Hoggett caught in the act this time, it would prove that his dad had nothing to do with the machine breakers and save Stanton's mill

– and all their jobs – at the same time!

The first person he thought of was Clara. She'd know what to do – but that meant getting into Stanton's Mill to find her. Thankfully, over the years, Charlie had found the perfect way to climb over the mill wall, even in daylight.

He ran back through the town, his heart thumping. He slipped along the wall to a place where some of the bricks had half-cracked, leaving foot- and handholds that he could use to scramble up. In a flash he was over the top and dropping down into the mill grounds.

He made his way to the big house, being careful not to be seen. The apple tree outside reached just high enough to touch Clara's window. Charlie put a handful of pebbles in his pocket and then began to climb.

When he got to the branch of the tree that was nearest Clara's window, he threw one stone, just hard enough for it to make a 'chinking' sound against the glass. Nothing happened, so he threw another, and then another.

"Come on, Clara," he whispered to himself. "I'm going to run out in a minute! You have to be there!"

It took another two pebbles before Clara's face appeared, and she threw the window open.

"What are you doing here?" she hissed. "If my father catches you you'll end up in a jail cell, for sure. You'll be sent off to Australia along with your father!"

"Just be quiet and listen for once," Charlie ordered her, and then explained what he'd found out. Clara's eyes got rounder and rounder as he talked.

"Oh no," she said. "What are we going to do?"

"Can't you talk to your pa again?" Charlie asked. "If you tell him what we know now…"

Clara shook her head. "I don't think he will listen. He's so angry – even with me."

"Well, what about the police then?" Charlie suggested. "They would want to stop the crime."

"Only if they believe you, Charlie," Clara pointed out. "No, I think it's up to us. We have to stop this ourselves!"

"We won't be able to do that," insisted Charlie. "We need help."

Clara crossed her arms and raised her chin.

Chapter 9

Midnight Adventure

"No one's going to help us, Charlie," Clara insisted. "You know that! Every time we've tried to tell someone what we know so far, we've just got into more trouble. If you want to prove your dad is innocent, we have to stop the machine breakers ourselves!"

Charlie felt his shoulders slump. He knew she was right. He just wished she wasn't. "It's too dangerous," he said.

Clara shook her head. "It'll be fine," she said, her eyes shining with excitement.

"All we need to do is be there on the road before the breakers. We can warn the machine carriers, and no one will get hurt. I'll meet you at our usual place at seven o'clock tonight."

"That's hours away!" said Charlie.

"They're not bringing the machine in until really late tonight," Clara reminded him. "Go on, go – quick, before someone sees you!"

Charlie did as he was told. The rest of the afternoon passed in a whirl of anxiety. Charlie felt as if he had a whole army of elephants stomping around in his stomach. Several times he thought about just going to the police station and blurting it all out. But deep down, he knew Clara was right. This was down to them.

At 7 pm, Charlie was crouched inside their oak tree, waiting for Clara. Time ticked by, and he began to think that she wasn't coming. Then he heard a sound in the wintery gloom ahead. He peeked out of his hiding place to see Clara leading a horse towards him, a small lantern glowing in the darkness.

"Clara!" Charlie said as he shot out of his hiding place and then stopped and stared. "What are you wearing?" he gasped, giggling.

Clara was dressed in baggy woollen trousers, old boots and a boy's shirt and jacket. Her long hair had been stuffed under a boy's cap. She looked down at herself and grinned with a shrug. "They're old things of William's," she said. "I had to cut the bottoms off the trousers, but they're so much easier to ride in than a stupid skirt! Come on, we'd better go. Rufus won't mind taking us both."

"Rufus?" Charlie asked.

"The pony, of course," Clara said, with a sigh. "You didn't think we were going to walk all the way to Markwell Cross, did you? It's more than seven miles away!"

* * *

It began to rain as they trotted up and out of the town. The drops were full of ice as if they really wanted to be snow, but couldn't quite manage it. The road was dark and the two children didn't speak much. Charlie knew Clara was as nervous as he was, though of course she'd never admit it.

They reached Markwell Cross, but there was no sign of anyone else there. Clara pointed down one of the roads that stretched away into the night. "The Mowton road. That's the way the carriers are coming. We'll just have to keep riding until we see them. We can get them to take another route into town."

They'd gone another two miles before they saw a cart coming towards them. Two men were sitting on the front, driving it, and two more were walking ahead, carrying oil lamps to light the way. They stopped when they saw the horse approaching.

"Who's there?" One of the men shouted. "Reveal yourselves!"

"We're friends!" Charlie shouted back. "From Stanton's Mill!"

"You're just children," he said. "What are you playing at?"

"Nothing," said Charlie. "We've come to warn you. There are breakers up ahead, waiting to ambush you at the Cross."

The men looked suspicious. "Oh yes? And old Stanton thought he'd send a couple of ragamuffins out to tell us about it, did he? You're pulling my leg, lad."

"No!" Clara exclaimed. "We're not joking – you've got to listen to us!"

"I don't '*got*' to do anything," said the man. "I know what you two are about. You've been sent by the breakers to lead us right into a trap."

"That's not true!" Charlie shouted.

"Well, I guess we'll find out soon enough, won't we?" The man hesitated for a moment, and then turned to his companions. "Get the clubs out. If there's any trouble, let's be prepared this time."

The men produced large wooden clubs from the cart. Charlie felt a bit sick when he thought about what they might be used for.

"Move on," the man said, to the cart driver. "We've got a schedule to keep."

"Wait – please," said Charlie. "We're not lying!"

"Out of the way, lad," said the man.

"What are we going to do?" Clara asked, as the cart rumbled on down the road.

"Let's ride ahead of them," said Charlie. "Maybe we can scare the breakers off!"

Clara urged Rufus into a trot, heading back towards Markwell Cross. When they got closer they saw that a group of four or five men were now blocking the road. They carried burning torches that lit their angry faces with orange-yellow flickers of flame light. Right in the middle of the line was Jack Hoggett.

Chapter 10

Good News… at Last

Clara sat high on her horse, facing down the gang of ruffians.

"The carriers are on their way… and they're armed!" she shouted, as loudly and bravely as she could. "Go back home and there won't be any trouble!"

"Oh yeah?" shouted back Hoggett. "Who cares if they're armed? So are we!"

"The constables are on their way, too," Charlie shouted, to the breakers. "You'll be arrested if they find you here."

"I don't believe you!"

"It's true!" Charlie lied, "They know that Mercer sent you to ambush Mr Stanton's machine at the Cross."

The breakers looked at each other, obviously worried by this. "Here, how does he know the plan?" one asked Hoggett.

"Be quiet!" said Hoggett. "He's bluffing."

Charlie looked back over his shoulder to see the cart following close behind. "We know who you are," he yelled again. "And even if you manage to destroy the machine, you'll never get away with it this time!"

There was a yell from behind as the machine carriers saw what was happening. They left the cart and began to run towards the breakers, shouting loudly.

"Sorry, Jack!" said one of the breakers as he dropped his torch on the ground and began to run. The others followed, charging back down the road, their boots churning up the cold mud.

"They're getting away!" Clara shouted, as Jack Hoggett turned and followed suit.

Charlie leapt from Rufus's back and hurtled after his fleeing figure. If he didn't stop Hoggett now, they'd never be able to prove his dad was innocent!

"Charlie!" Clara yelled, scared, "be careful!"

Charlie flung himself at the man, catching Hoggett around the knees and sending them both sprawling. The breaker tried to scramble up, but Charlie held on to his legs.

"Get off me, you little–"

Hoggett tried to kick at him, but Charlie clung on like a limpet. He heard the sound of heavy footsteps and suddenly a large figure loomed over them. Someone grabbed Hoggett by the shoulder.

"Don't worry, lad," said the machine carrier. "We've got him now. It's all over – thanks to you."

Things happened very quickly after that. The carriers tied Jack Hoggett up. They put him in the cart with the machine and then they all carried on to Stanton's Mill together. Before they got there, Clara nudged Charlie.

"I've got to get back into my own clothes," she whispered. "If father catches me like this, I'll be in *real* trouble!"

Charlie squeezed her hand. "Thanks for your help," he said. "I couldn't have done it without you, Clara."

Clara grinned and squeezed back. "My pleasure," she said. "It was a real adventure!"

Charlie slipped from Rufus' back and gave the horse a pat before Clara rode him into the night.

Mr Stanton was waiting for the carriers when they reached the mill – but he hadn't been expecting the story that they had to tell him. Once he'd heard everything, he disappeared for a few minutes – "To send a message or two", he said. Charlie was waiting patiently in the hallway with the others when Clara appeared at the top of the stairs. Now wearing a long nightgown, she winked at him cheekily as her father returned.

"Well, well, well," said Mr Stanton, raising his eyebrows at Charlie. "We meet again master Thwaite. And this time, I hear I've got you to thank for saving my machine."

"It wasn't just me, Mr Stanton," Charlie began, glancing at Clara, "I had help from–" he stopped when he saw Clara, now standing behind her dad, shaking her head frantically. "Er – from someone else," he finished, lamely.

"Ah yes, this other boy the carriers told me about. Who is he?"

"Um…" said Charlie, not sure what to say. "Well–"

"Does it really matter, father?" Clara asked. "All that's really important is that Charlie's not the troublemaker you thought he was. He saved the machine!"

"That's true," said Mr Stanton, nodding. "Even though I had already dismissed you. That shows true loyalty and strength of character. I am most grateful to you, my boy."

"I…I did it for my dad," Charlie said, quietly. "I wanted to prove that he was innocent… that he didn't have anything to do with the first breaking. He shouldn't be in jail, Mr Stanton. He was set up by Hoggett."

"Yes, I realize that now," nodded the mill owner. "Don't worry, I've already sent word that he's to be released immediately. And there'll be a job for him at the mill as long as he wants it. For you, too, if you've a mind to come back."

"A job?" Charlie repeated, astonished. "But – but I thought that the machine meant you didn't need as many workers any more?"

"Don't need the workers?" Stanton asked, a puzzled frown wrinkling his brow. "Is that what you all thought? Well, perhaps if I had made this clearer earlier, we wouldn't have got into this mess in the first place. It won't be replacing any workers, Charlie, just one of the old machines. It's a better model, you see – faster, cleaner and more reliable. It'll mean I can take on more work, so, in the long run, the mill's just going to get busier and I'll need *more* workers. That's got to be good for everyone, hasn't it?"

Charlie nodded "Yes, Mr Stanton. That sounds very good indeed."

"Now tell me – is it true that Mercer was behind all this?" the mill owner asked.

"Yes," replied Charlie, eagerly. "I saw him talking to Hoggett – telling him to break the machine. He said he wanted to put you out of business, sir."

"Well, now he's going to have to answer to the law," said Stanton, smartly. "And it will be *him* going out of business… which will mean even more work for Stanton's, I suppose."

"Yes, sir!" said Charlie, beaming.

"Right, well it's late and I'd better get some sleep. Thank you all for your good work. We'll expect to see you back at the mill tomorrow, Charlie," the mill owner said, heading towards the stairs. "Good night."

"Good night, sir," Charlie called after him.

"Well done, Charlie," said Clara, giving him a quick hug before hurrying after her dad.

* * *

It was almost dawn by the time Charlie walked home. The rain had stopped, and although it was still cold, it looked as if it was going to be a beautiful day. As he turned into his street, he saw two policemen outside his house.

For a moment Charlie froze, scared. Then he ran up to his door, threw it open and dashed inside. There was his dad, hugging Liza, Jim and Flora all at once.

"Pa!" He shouted, overjoyed. "They let you go!"

His dad gently pulled away from the rest of the family and smiled at Charlie. "Yes, lad, they did," he said, grabbing him in a bear-like embrace. "And it's all down to you, you clever boy. What you did was very dangerous, you know."

Charlie hugged his dad back, hard. "It was worth it, dad," he said. "It was all worth it."

THE END

FICTION EXPRESS

THE READERS TAKE CONTROL!

Have you ever wanted to change the course of a plot, change a character's destiny, tell an author what to write next?

Well, now you can!

'Threads' was originally written for the award-winning interactive e-book website Fiction Express.

Fiction Express e-books are published in gripping weekly episodes. At the end of each episode, readers are given voting options to decide where the plot goes next. They vote online and the winning vote is then conveyed to the author who writes the next episode, in real time, according to the readers' most popular choice.

www.fictionexpress.co.uk

WINNER
Education Resources
Award for Innovation

FICTION EXPRESS

TALK TO THE AUTHORS

The Fiction Express website features a blog where readers can interact with the authors while they are writing. An exciting and unique opportunity!

FANTASTIC TEACHER RESOURCES

Each weekly Fiction Express episode comes with a PDF of teacher resources packed with ideas to extend the text.

"The teaching resources are fab and easily fill a whole week of literacy lessons!"
Rachel Humphries, teacher at Westacre Middle School

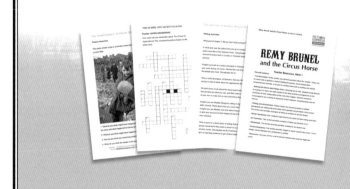

FICTI●N EXPRESS

The Time Detectives: The Mystery of Maddie Musgrove by Alex Woolf

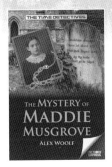

When Joe Smallwood goes to stay with his Uncle Theo and cousin Maya life seems dull until he finds a strange smartphone nestling beside a gravestone. The phone enables Joe and Maya to become time-travelling detectives and takes them on an exciting adventure back to Victorian times. Can they save innocent maidservant Maddie Musgrove from the gallows?

ISBN 978-1-78322-459-3

The Time Detectives: The Disappearance of Danny Doyle by Alex Woolf

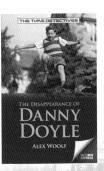

When the Time Detectives, Joe and Maya, stumble upon an old house in the middle of a wood, its occupant has a sad and strange tale to tell. Michael was evacuated to Dorset during World War II with his twin brother, Danny. While there, Danny mysteriously disappeared and was never heard from again. Can Joe and Maya succeed where the police failed, journey back to 1941 and trace Michael's missing brother?

ISBN 978-1-78322-458-6

FICTION EXPRESS

My Cousin Faustina
by Bea Davenport

Jez is horrified to find a strange girl sitting in his kitchen when he gets home from school. His parents claim she is a distant cousin, but Jez senses something odd about her. Just what dark secret is Faustina hiding?

In his quest to find out, Jez learns the true value of family and friendship.

ISBN 978-1-78322-539-2

FICTION EXPRESS

The Pirate's Secret
by Stewart Ross

One windswept winter's evening Arden Tregorey listens enthralled as his father tells him of his 'golden secret' and of how he once outwitted the notorious one-eared pirate Lambert 'Luggole' Spain. The very next day his father is kidnapped and disappears, so young Arden decides to set off to the Caribbean in search of him.

But how will he travel the 5000 miles of dangerous Atlantic Ocean, and will he succeed in finding his only living relative?

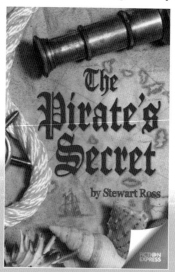

ISBN 978-1-78322-552-1

FICTI●N EXPRESS

Rémy Brunel and the Circus Horse
by Sharon Gosling

"Roll up, roll up, and see the greatest show on Earth!" Rémy Brunel loves her life in the circus – riding elephants, practising tightrope tricks and dazzling audiences. But when two new magicians arrive at the circus, everyone is wary of them. What exactly are they up to? What secrets are they trying to hide? Should Rémy and her new friend Matthias trust them?

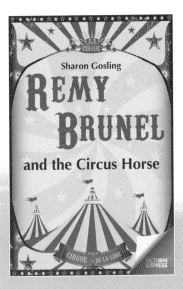

ISBN 978-1-78322-469-2

About the Author

Sharon and her husband live in a remote village in northern England, surrounded by fells and sheep. When she's not writing, she bakes a lot of cakes and bread, attempts to grow things in an allotment, and catches the baby rabbits unhelpfully brought in by the cat.